P9-CFJ-607

DATE DUE

DEMCO 38-296

SEVEN SCARY MONSTERS

BY MARY BETH LUNDGREN

ILLUSTRATED BY
HOWARD FINE

CLARION BOOKS / NEW YORK

Clarion Books
a Houghton Mifflin Company imprint
215 Park Avenue South, New York, NY 10003
Text copyright © 2003 by Mary Beth Lundgren
Illustrations copyright © 2003 by Howard Fine

The illustrations were executed in pastel.
The text was set in 21-point Ad Lib.

www.houghtonmifflinbooks.com

Printed in Singapore.

Library of Congress Cataloging in Publication Data
Lundgren, Mary Beth.
Seven scary monsters / by Mary Beth Lundgren ; illustrated by Howard Fine.
p. cm.
Summary: At bedtime, a little boy vanquishes the seven monsters that
inhabit his room and tells them not to come back.
ISBN 0-395-88913-8 (alk. paper)
[1. Monsters—Fiction. 2. Bedtime—Fiction. 3. Stories in rhyme.] I. Fine, Howard, ill. II. Title.
PZ8.3.L9725 Se 2002
[E] 21
2001054790
TWP 10 9 8 7 6 5 4 3 2 1

To Mom and Dad, who taught me to love—even monsters

—M. B. L.

For my children and all their scary monsters

—H. F.

SEVEN scary monsters hiding in my room.

One groans and glares—*EEEEK!*
—sneaking closer . . .

4

BOOM!

I trap it in my monster box.

"Quick!" I holler. "Snap the locks!

"Rick! **Rack! Wrinkleshack!**
Don't you dare come back!"

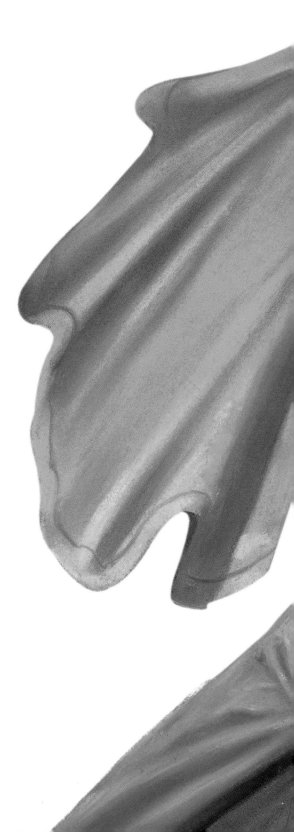

7

SIX scary monsters

leafing through my books.

One **RIIIPPPPS** a page.

"Hey, careful with your hooks!"

My monster vacuum slurps.

I smile.

THWOMP! It's on the compost pile.

"Rick! Rack! Wrinkleshack!
Don't you dare come back!"

FIVE scary monsters swimming with my fishes.

One bares its teeth. Good grief, its grin is vicious.

My monster-catching purple felines
fling it—*SPLAT!*—among the pea vines.

"Rick! **Rack! Wrinkleshack!**
Don't you dare come back!"

16

FOUR scary monsters crashing my computer. One chomps a file. I load my monster shooter.

17

18

Ignition! Power up! Energize!
"ZAP!" I yell. "You're atomized!

"Rick! Rack! Wrinkleshack!
Don't you dare come back!"

THREE scary monsters
whisper by my door.
One twirls and slips— *YOW!*
Wow, that thing can roar!

My monster-magnetizing wand
drops it—*PLOP!*—beyond the pond.

"Rick! **Rack! Wrinkleshack!**
Don't you dare come back!"

TWO scary monsters
pounce on my giraffe.
One nips his neck—*OUCH!*
—then whoops a loony laugh.

I blast it with my monster spray.

"Out!" I shout. "Now back away!

"Rick! Rack! Wrinkleshack!
Don't you dare come back!"

ONE scary monster
swinging from the ceiling fan,
chatters like a chimp. But this is no orangutan.
"Go home!" I yell. "I called your dad.
See? It's dark, and—*WOW!*—he's mad.

"Rick! **Rack! Wrinkleshack!**
Don't you dare come back!"

No more scary monsters
hiding in my room.

Can't sleep. Too quiet. Too much elbowroom.

"Guys!" I shout. "I'm really sorry.

I'll read your favorite monster story.

"Rick! Rack! Wrinkleshack!

"Monsters,
    please come back!"